THE HOUSE IN THE MAIL

BY ROSEMARY AND TOM WELLS

ILLUSTRATED BY DAN ANDREASEN

VIKING

Hello, whoever you are out there in the world of the future! I wonder how many years will pass before someone reads this. I'm only twelve years old now, but I might be a very old lady by the time you read these pages.

Let me introduce myself. I am Emily Cartwright of Enfield, Kentucky. I was born in the south bedroom of Gran and Grandad's house on March 16, 1916. March is cold and rainy, and the south bed-room was a touch warmer than the north bedroom.

Homer, my brother, came along in August three years later. Ma had Homer in the north bedroom because it was cooler in there.

We had just those two bedrooms, one for Gran and Grandad, and one for Ma and Pa. Homer and I slept up in the attic. That was fine when I was five and Homer just as big as a minute.

But when we were nine and six years old, Homer got a spider collection going. Then a snakeskin collection and live frogs.

And when I got to be eleven I shot up so tall I couldn't stand in the attic anymore. We were running out of room.

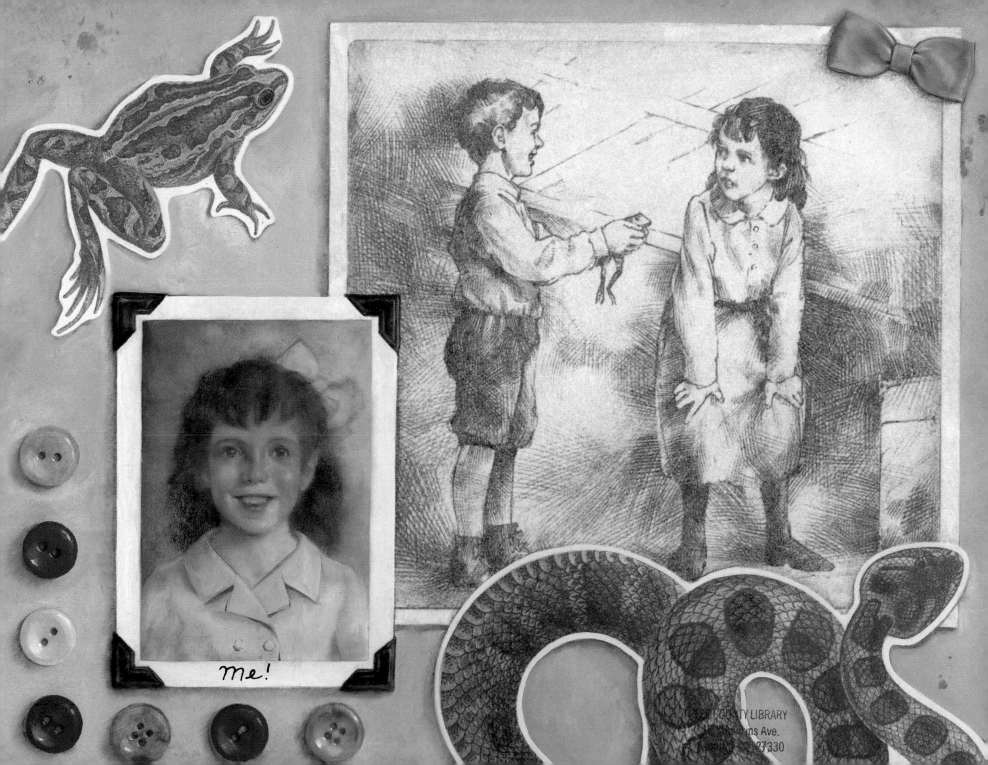

me!

I'll never forget the night I first heard about the house in the mail. At supper I told everyone I never wanted to look at another spider or frog as long as I lived. I was going to take the train to Chicago and move in with Aunt Cecilia permanently because Homer had stolen my perfect robin's egg, my silver dollar, and the gold ring with the glass ruby that I won at the state fair. I found all of my treasures in the dust under Homer's bed.

me on the pony ride at the state fair last summer

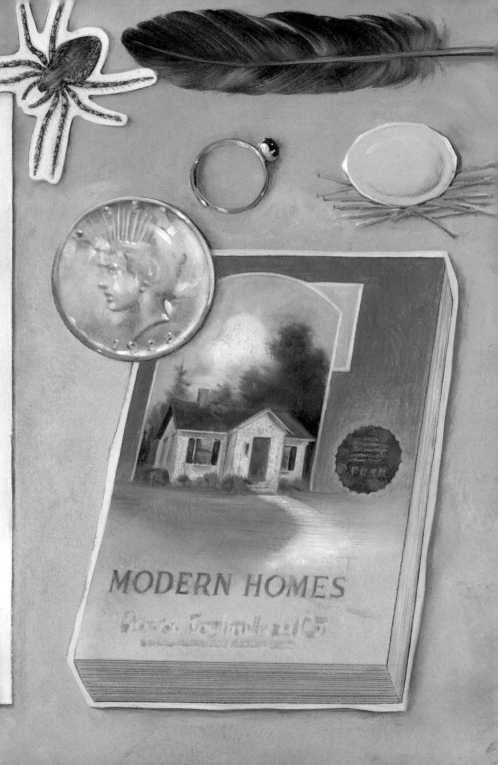

MODERN HOMES

"Emily," said Ma, "you're right. We do live tight as bees in a hive. But we are about to build a new house of our very own, with a room for each of you and one for the new baby."

"What new baby?" Homer and I both asked at once.

"Either Joseph or Josephine Cartwright will join us come the first frost," said Pa. Then he slapped a big fat catalog onto the kitchen table. It was filled with pictures of houses big, little, and in-between. They had wonderful names like the Marvina, the Worthington, and the Carthage.

"Every house in this book comes in a put-together kit," Pa explained. "We'll pick up ours at the railroad depot in Lexington and put the whole thing together with a barrel of nails."

"You mean we get to choose a house out of all of these?" Homer asked.

"And they'll send it to us, just like that?" I said.

"That's right," said Ma.

There were so many houses to choose from, and each house was different. Ma wanted one with a porch, like the Beckford. Homer liked the Jefferson. "I could crawl out my bedroom window and watch the stars from the roof," he said. Pa liked the look of the Carlisle, with its big kitchen and front pillars. Finally, we found one we could all agree on—the Lincoln.

It had a porch for Ma and a window onto the roof for Homer and the big kitchen Pa liked. As for me, I was going to have my very own bedroom.

"Can I have a secret compartment for my treasures built into my room?" I whispered to Pa.

"We'll see," Pa said. He wrote out a check to Sears, Roebuck & Company for $2,500—the price of the Lincoln.

"That represents our whole life savings," said Ma.

That night Homer and I lay down in our side-by-side beds. Homer grumped, "I wish they'd bought a brand-new Ford truck with all that money."

"Homer," I pointed out, "you've got less sense than one of your frogs. The new house is going to have a gas stove. No more wood for you to chop and carry in. An electric refrigerator. No more drip pan for you to empty from under the icebox. And Ma won't make you carry twenty buckets of hot water for the laundry, because we're getting a new washing machine. Think with your brain, Homer."

Homer said, "But it's got running water indoors. That means Ma will make me take more baths, instead of just Saturday night."

FASTEST IN THE WORLD

A touch of the toe empties the tank.

Modern

The first thing we had to do to build the house was dig a great big hole in the ground. Pa had a level spot staked out in one of Grandad's front pastures. Our neighbor, Will Cox, was pleased to lend us his draft horse to help with the work.

Pa and Will and Will's horse, Dolly, pulled boulders as big as motorcars out of the ground. They split them up to make walls for the foundation.

"Why?" asked Homer.

"The foundation spreads the weight of the house on the soil down deep enough so the frost won't heave it," Pa explained.

Deep in the hole, Pa and Will mixed a mortar of cement, sand, and water, thick as oatmeal, in an old wheelbarrow. They pieced the rock wall together, using the mortar to fill the spaces in between. When the mortar set, not a pebble of that wall would ever move again. Homer and I fetched buckets of water until we thought our arms would fall off.

Buckets in the Grass
by Emily Cartwright

On the first day of May, we all went down to the Lexington railroad depot. Half the town showed up to see the house come in. It filled a railroad car all on its own. Everyone helped with the loading and unloading. It took three trips in Grandad's old pickup truck to get it all home.

You can't drive nails into rock, so the first boards that went on the foundation wall had big holes drilled into them to match the bolts that Pa had cemented into the top of the wall. Everything else in the whole house is nailed to something that's nailed to one of those boards.

By May 10, the subfloor was finished, flat enough to roller skate on.

Homer squirreled away all the leftover scraps of wood.

"What are you doing with all those wood scraps, Homer?" Pa asked.

Homer wouldn't tell. But I followed him way into the woods one evening. He was building a tree house where he could hide.

Train Coming! by Emily Cartwright

HOMER'S TREEHOUSE

It was time for the first four walls. The parlor, dining room, and kitchen walls were nailed together in panels flat on the floor, then raised upright. Ma made lemonade by the gallon to keep us all going in the hot sun.

My job was to keep the blueprint opened flat and read the measurements to Pa and Will. Will marked lines on the wood with snaps of a chalked string. Puffs of blue chalk dust blew away in the wind.

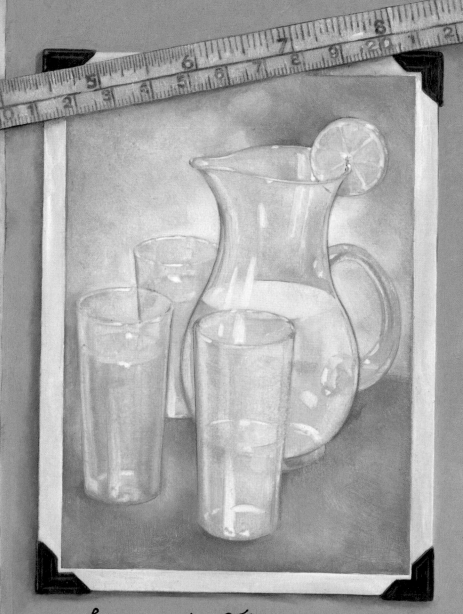

Lemonade Time
by Emily Cartwright

RAISING THE PARLOR WALL

On the Fourth of July, we took a day off and went into Lexington for the big celebration. There was a pic-nic, a parade, and fireworks. Will is a veteran of the Great War, and he marched in the parade wearing his uniform.

Next day, we started building the second floor.

"Where's my secret compartment, Pa?" I asked.

"It's a secret," said Pa.

Our friend Mike Pratt came over to help with the roof.

Three men hauled up the rafter boards that held up the roof. Sweat poured down like rain. They looked as if they had been dunked in the swimming hole. Ma used up two bottles of liniment on Pa's back and shoulders during the week it took to finish framing the roof.

August came. A black tar-paper blanket went over the roof boards. On this bed, slate shingles were nailed down, and the roof was snug and tight.

The outside of the house got a coat of stucco. Stucco goes on sticky and dries hard. It looks like icing swirls. Homer pushed his hand into the sandy stickiness down in back where Pa wouldn't see.

"Where's your tree house, Homer?" I teased him.

"No one will ever find it," said Homer.

Homer's Handprint by Emily Cartwright

"I already have," I said, and I turned a big cartwheel, which Homer couldn't do.

By month's end, we had a house all perfect on the outside.

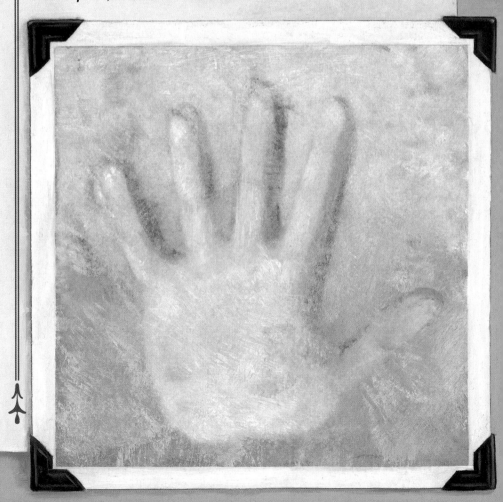

AUGUST 29, 1928

One night we ate supper in the backyard of our new house. The Pratts came and the Coxes and of course Gran and Grandad, too. We washed up the dishes with water from the pump as we always have.

"Clear the decks for modern times," said Pa. "The plumber's coming tomorrow. In a week's time, you'll turn on a tap and all the water in the world will run into your cup."

The moon rose over the dark old house and the dark new house together.

"Can you imagine electric light?" asked Ma.

Homer caught a jar of fireflies.

"This is the only light I am ever going to need," Homer declared to one and all.

Caught by
Emily Cartwright
summer
1928

Homer's Light
by Emily Cartwright

School started on September 7. Homer and I walked home every day to a new surprise. One day it was the plumbing pipe and drains. Then it was the electric wires all through the house. After that came the coal-burning furnace, and big round metal ducts to carry the warm air from the furnace to each room in the house.

A man named Clem came to plaster the inside walls. One day after the plaster was hard, Homer and I ran through the house singing. Our songs echoed from room to room like loud voices on the radio.

Smooth, yellow pine boards were nailed down to the subfloor. The hammering sounded like gunshots.

The kitchen floor linoleum wouldn't stay flat, so Homer and I stood on one end until Pa could tack it down.

Twenty-two doors were hung on brass hinges.

"Where's my secret compartment, Pa?" I asked one night, but Pa smiled and shook his head.

"Emily, I just forgot where I put it."

The stairs went in, and Clem came back to help with the painting. Suddenly a Hoosier cabinet appeared in the kitchen. Then the stove and refrigerator and washing machine. No more ashes for me to carry out of the stove. Never again would I have to help Ma, leaning over the old laundry tub to scrub clothes.

"Guess what!" Ma said.

"What?" I asked.

"We can keep the ice cream more than a couple of hours now. It'll keep as long as we want in the freezer compartment."

ICE COLD

MA, SEVEN MONTHS ALONG

Our First Dinner in the New House

At the end of October, Ma made apple cider instead of lemonade, and the house was finished. After supper Pa put his finger to his lips and beckoned me to follow him. On the floor of my clothes closet he pushed on a knot, and the board came up! Under the board was my secret compartment! I put in my robin's egg, my silver dollar, and my ruby ring. When I put back the board no one could ever know.

Pa's self-portrait

PUSH

0

I was the first Cartwright to take a bubble bath in a real bathroom with hot water splashing right into my toes.

On November 5, 1927, Joseph Cartwright was born in the hospital in Lexington. He was the first member of the family ever born away from home.

Joseph's room has the slippery smell of new paint and the Christmassy smell of pine beams. Pa bathes Joseph in the brand-new kitchen sink. Ma warms his supper on the brand-new gas stove. Joseph is going to grow up in the modern world, and he'll never know how it was in the old days.

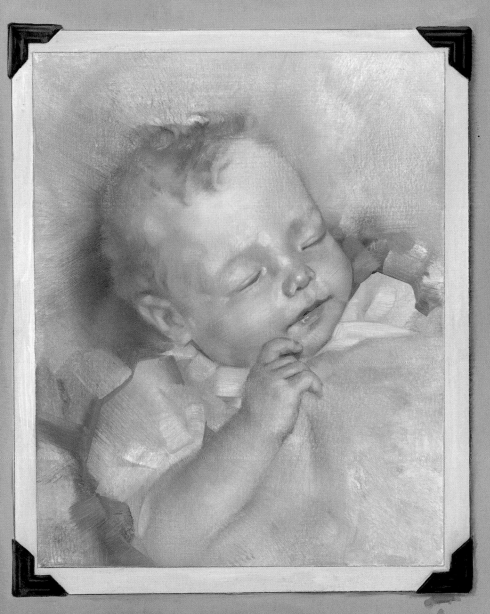

Joseph Cartwright, one week

GUERIN'S FURNITURE

SALE

Special Delivery

But Homer and I…we sit
wrapped in blankets in
Homer's tree house under
the Kentucky stars, and
we remember.

VIKING
Published by the Penguin Group
Penguin Putnam Books for Young Readers,
345 Hudson Street, New York, New York 10014, U.S.A.
Penguin Books Ltd, 80 Strand, London WC2R 0RL, England
Penguin Books Australia Ltd, Ringwood, Victoria, Australia
Penguin Books Canada Ltd, 10 Alcorn Avenue, Toronto, Ontario, Canada M4V 3B2
Penguin Books (N.Z.) Ltd, 182-190 Wairau Road, Auckland 10, New Zealand

Penguin Books Ltd, Registered Offices: Harmondsworth, Middlesex, England

First published in 2002 by Viking, a division of Penguin Putnam Books for Young Readers.

1 2 3 4 5 6 7 8 9 10

Text copyright © Rosemary and Tom Wells, 2002
Illustrations copyright © Dan Andreasen, 2002
All rights reserved

Library of Congress Cataloging-in-Publication Data is available.
ISBN 0-670-03545-9
Printed in Singapore by Imago
Set in Electra Cursive

E
Wells
The house in the mail